Does she still think she's a poodle?
Or is she a Great Dane again?

She's purring!

And another for Helen

Pinkerton, are you lonely? Do you miss curling
up with your brothers and sisters?

We should get some other Great Dane puppies
to play with Pinkerton.

I think he's trying to tell you that he agrees with me.

One Great Dane is enough! The only other pet I would consider would be something small and quiet…like a goldfish.

I'll go find a friend for you, Pinkerton.

BUS STOP

This is the perfect place!

Pinkerton couldn't curl up with a goldfish.

And he couldn't play with a bird.

Maybe a kitten would be just right!

It says here in my book that Great Dane puppies
and kittens can become good friends.

Here's a surprise for you and Pinkerton.
Her name is Rose.

It says in this book by Sarah Chattercat that Great
Dane puppies and kittens can become good friends.

He seems to like her.

Rose took over Pinkerton's sun spot.

She's eating his dinner.

I think Rose wants to be a Great Dane.

Oh, no!

Now Pinkerton is trying to be a kitten!

Let's go back to that pet show! I have a few questions for Sarah Chattercat!

Rose! Come back!

Pinkerton will be safe with the kittens.

Help me find Rose.

Rose! Where are you?

I see her! She's in line for the Grand March of the Poodles!

I'd like to welcome our television audience to this stunning event and to introduce Dr. Aleasha Kibble of Canine University, who will present the Golden Poodle Trophy.

Stop the ceremony! Call the police! The Grand March has been infiltrated by a feline impostor!

Excuse us, but that's our cat, Rose. She used to think she was a Great Dane but she's decided to be a poodle.

Ladies and gentlemen, the crowd and the poodles have gone berserk!

They are chasing the intruding cat toward the Castle of the Kittens!

There's a monster in the Castle of the Kittens.

Arrest that brute! He terrified our poodles, and they've all fainted!

Nonsense! This wonderful dog saved the kittens.
He's a hero!

Look! It's Rose!